# The Heron Princess

△△△△△△△△△△

Don't miss Emma and Martín's previous legendary adventures!

*Wrath of the Rain God*
*The Beginning of All Things*
*The Child King of Uxmal*

# The Heron Princess

By Karla Arenas Valenti
Illustrated by Vanessa Morales

## Aladdin
NEW YORK   AMSTERDAM/ANTWERP   LONDON
TORONTO   SYDNEY/MELBOURNE   NEW DELHI

This book is a work of fiction. Any references to historical events, real people, or real places are used fictitiously. Other names, characters, places, and events are products of the author's imagination, and any resemblance to actual events or places or persons, living or dead, is entirely coincidental.

ALADDIN
An imprint of Simon & Schuster Children's Publishing Division
1230 Avenue of the Americas, New York, New York 10020
First Aladdin hardcover edition April 2025
Text copyright © 2025 by Karla Valenti
Illustrations copyright © 2025 by Vanessa Morales
Also available in an Aladdin paperback edition.
All rights reserved, including the right of reproduction in whole or in part in any form.
ALADDIN and related logo are registered trademarks of Simon & Schuster, LLC.
For information about special discounts for bulk purchases, please contact Simon & Schuster Special Sales at 1-866-506-1949 or business@simonandschuster.com.
The Simon & Schuster Speakers Bureau can bring authors to your live event. For more information or to book an event contact the Simon & Schuster Speakers Bureau at 1-866-248-3049 or visit our website at www.simonspeakers.com.
Designed by Tiara Iandiorio
The illustrations for this book were rendered digitally.
The text of this book was set in Gitan Latin.
Manufactured in the United States of America 0125 BVG
2 4 6 8 10 9 7 5 3 1
Library of Congress Cataloging-in-Publication Data
Names: Valenti, Karla, author. | Morales, Vanessa, illustrator.
Title: The heron princess / by Karla Arenas Valenti ; illustrated by Vanessa Morales.
Description: First Aladdin paperback edition. | New York : Aladdin, 2025. |
Series: Legendarios ; 4 | Audience term: Preteens | Audience: Ages 7 to 10. |
Summary: Twins Emma and Martín, along with their abuela, embark on a magical adventure in the book of legends, where they must help Princess Hapunda defend her village from an enemy tribe demanding her surrender.
Identifiers: LCCN 2024037568 (print) | LCCN 2024037569 (ebook) | ISBN 9781665936095 (paperback) | ISBN 9781665936088 (hardcover) | ISBN 9781665936101 (ebook)
Subjects: CYAC: Twins—Fiction. | Siblings—Fiction. | Magic—Fiction. | Books—Fiction. | Mexican Americans—Fiction. | Fantasy. | LCGFT: Fantasy fiction. | Novels.
Classification: LCC PZ7.1.V336 He 2025 (print) | LCC PZ7.1.V336 (ebook) | DDC [Fic]—dc23
LC record available at https://lccn.loc.gov/2024037568

# Contents

Chapter 1: Party Favors and Perfectionism
**1**

Chapter 2: Dad's Nugget of Wisdom
**9**

Chapter 3: The Heron Princess
**19**

Chapter 4: A Mysterious Lake
**25**

Chapter 5: The Power of Pátzcuaro
**33**

Chapter 6: The Love Story
**39**

Chapter 7: Danger Approaches
**46**

Chapter 8: The Right-Size Bubble
**53**

Chapter 9: Trapped!
**63**

Chapter 10: A Plan Interrupted
**71**

Chapter 11: Some Handy Wizardry
**81**

Chapter 12: Tick, Tick, Tick
**91**

Chapter 13: A Giant Whirlpool!
**104**

Chapter 14: A Feathery Transformation
**112**

Chapter 15: Same but Different
**119**

Chapter 16: Lesson Learned
**127**

Author's Note
**135**

△△△△△△△△△△

To Anna Parsons and the wonderful team at Aladdin and S&S who helped me bring this marvelous series to life

▽▽▽▽▽▽▽▽▽▽

# Party Favors and Perfectionism

Sitting in the back seat of his friend's mom's car, Martín shoved a handful of sour gummies into his mouth. His tongue tingled.

"Here we are." His friend's mom parked in front of Martín's house.

"Thank you, Mrs. Porter," Martín mumbled between sticky chews.

"You are most welcome," she replied. "It

looks like you boys had a great time."

Martín and his friend Henry were covered in confetti, which was plastered to their faces by sweat.

"Laser tag was *awesome!*" Henry said, and gave Martín a fist bump.

"Bye!" Martín stepped out of the car. He laughed as the car pulled away with Henry's chocolate-smeared face smooshed against the window making silly faces.

Martín hadn't expected to make friends so quickly.

In Mexico, he'd had one friend, a great friend! Arturo. Martín had never really connected that much with his other classmates. And anyway, Arturo was awesome, so it suited him just fine. Martín's twin sister, Emma, was the social one, the one who never had trouble meeting new people.

But for some reason, Martín had found it

a lot easier to make friends in his new school here in the US. Everyone was so friendly, and there were so many activities and fun things to do in school and after school. Martín had signed up for every activity he could, and he even enjoyed his classes.

He was good in PE and always had people to eat lunch with. Before he knew it, everyone in the school seemed to know who he was.

It was weird. And not just because he had a ton of friends. It was weird because the exact opposite seemed to have happened with Emma.

She had made exactly zero friends. In Mexico, Emma was always surrounded by friends and talking nonstop. Mami even had to set a phone time limit because Emma would spend hours chatting with her friends.

Now, though, his sister hardly ever talked to anyone. She didn't join any of the after-school activities (even though Martín knew there were some Emma would love!). She always sat alone at lunch. Emma didn't even want to go to the birthday party she just got invited to. She said the only reason she was even invited was because people felt bad for her because she was the new kid but that they didn't *really* want to be her friend.

Martín wasn't sure that was true. He thought that maybe she was worried they wouldn't like her. But it hardly mattered anyway. A party was a party. What better way to make friends than chasing after each other with laser guns for an hour?

He reached into his goodie bag as he stepped into the house.

"Not until after dinner!" Mami called out to him from the kitchen. It was like she had X-ray vision!

She came out to greet him, and even

though she was smiling, Martín knew she was serious about the candy. He put it back into his bag and swallowed the remainder of his sour gummies.

"How was the party?" Abuela asked. She had arrived the day before from Mexico for a visit and would be staying for a week.

"It was great," he told her.

Next to Abuela on the couch, Emma rolled her eyes. She had started doing that *a lot* lately.

"Of course it was," Emma said. "You think *everything* here is great."

"Well..." He sort of did.

"Anyway." Emma turned to Abuela. "As I was saying, school is terrible. The classes are so boring, and everyone is really mean."

"Are they really?" Abuela asked. "Didn't you just get invited to your classmate's birthday party?"

"Well, maybe not mean. But they can't

understand me when I talk; they sometimes laugh at how I say things."

Martín knew that part was true. He and his sister both had pretty strong Spanish accents, and they didn't always pronounce things the way others did. It didn't bother Martín, but Emma was a "perfectionist."

He'd recently learned that word, and it described his sister exactly. She was someone who wanted everything to be perfect. And when it wasn't, it stressed her out. Which was tough when you expected *yourself* to be perfect because, well, nobody was perfect.

Emma was so worried about doing everything right and fitting in perfectly that she wasn't doing anything right and wasn't fitting in at all. The problem was all the worrying!

Abuela put her hand on Emma's shoulder and said, "So, what do you like about being here?"

Emma sighed. "I like Nacho." The dog

looked up from where he had been sleeping on the carpet.

"I like Nacho too," Abuela said. The dog began happily wagging his tail.

"But that's the only thing," Emma said, and she crossed her arms.

"Abuela," Martín said, hoping to move the conversation into something more interesting. "I brought you something from the party." He held out a pair of earrings.

"You got earrings at a party?"

"They're not real," Martín told her. "But they glow in the dark. That was the theme of the party."

"Oh." She studied them closely. "Well, they're lovely. Thank you."

Abuela promptly clipped them onto her earlobes. Martín thought they looked a bit funny on his grandmother's ancient ears, and Emma must have agreed because she started giggling.

Abuela didn't mind, though. She smiled and peered into Martín's bag.

"What else do you have in there?"

"Some candies, a pencil, a super-bouncy ball."

"What is this?" Abuela poked at something shaped like a hand with a long sticky rope attached to it.

"Oh!" Martín pulled out the sticky rubber hand and smacked it onto the ceiling. Abuela burst out laughing.

"It's a sticky hand!" Martín grinned as he tugged at it and it smacked back at him.

"Yeah, that's great," Emma said. Martín could tell she was about to start complaining again. Fortunately, that was the exact moment when Dad walked in.

"Hola, mis amores!" he called out.

## Dad's Nugget of Wisdom

*Martín can be so annoying sometimes*, Emma thought. Especially now that he was one of the popular kids in school. How had *that* happened?

She scooped up a serving of mashed potatoes, maybe intentionally splattering some on Martín as she plopped the mash onto her plate.

"Ewww," he said, wiping a chunk of potato from his arm.

"Sorry," she mumbled. *Not sorry.*

She let a few peas roll off her spoon and onto his pants.

"Hey!" he cried.

"Ooops," Emma said.

When she reached for a slice of meat loaf, Martín scooted his chair out of the way, glaring at her as he did.

"What?" Emma asked in her most innocent voice.

Abuela raised an eyebrow at her, then turned to Martín. "So, when is your soccer match, Martín?" she asked.

"On Thursday. Are you coming?"

"I would love to," Abuela replied.

"We'll all be at the match," Dad said. "Don't worry."

That was another thing, Emma continued musing. Since when was Martín into sports? Real sports? Not the kind you played in a video game. From your bedroom. In your pajamas. Ever since they had moved to the US, he had suddenly "discovered" a love of sports. Basketball. Hockey. Now soccer.

"Blegh," Emma said.

"What's wrong with the meat loaf?" Mami asked.

"What?" Emma looked up.

"Do you not like the meat loaf?" Mami asked.

"Oh, no ... I was just thinking about something else," Emma replied.

*Something super annoying that used to be my twin brother and is now some weird version of a brother who I don't even know anymore.*

"What about you, Emma?" Abuela turned to her. "Do you have anything coming up this weekend that I could watch?"

"Yeah, right," Emma huffed. "There's nothing to do around here."

"That's not true at all," Mami said. "If

anything, there's not enough time for all the things you could do."

Emma knew Mami was right, but she definitely wasn't going to say so. Instead, she pushed her peas around her plate, jamming them into her mashed potatoes.

"I'm sure Emma will find something you can do with her," Dad added.

"Probably complain nonstop," Martín said under his breath.

Emma was calculating exactly how to get a forkful of mashed potatoes onto her brother's lap when Abuela said, "Well, I was actually hoping Emma and Martín would have time to read a story with me."

"A story?" Mami asked.

"A story!" Emma and Martín cried in unison.

"You want to read a story with them?" Dad had his I'm-so-confused face on, but Emma was not about to clarify.

"Yes!" Emma and Martín replied. Annoyingly, in unison once again. But Emma couldn't glare at her brother this time because she really did share his excitement.

Emma knew Abuela wasn't talking about an ordinary story. Abuela was referring to a book of legends she had given Emma and Martín as a parting gift when they moved from Mexico to the US. A *magical* book of legends.

Emma looked at Martín and nodded. It had been a long time since they had jumped into one of the stories. Emma had been so busy with schoolwork, and Martín always seemed to have an after-school club or sports practice or a playdate or a birthday party....

Emma was starting to get annoyed again.

"I was thinking since tomorrow is Sunday..." Abuela looked over at Emma and Martín, who both nodded vigorously.

After that Emma found it easier not to get

so annoyed with her brother for the remainder of dinner.

And she even kept her cool when Dad pulled her aside while they were clearing the table.

"I noticed you are particularly angry this evening," he told her.

She put on her most charming smile. "Why do you say that?"

Unfortunately, her dad was a middle school principal, and one of his superpowers was being able to see right through a kid's fake smile.

"So?" he said. "What's going on?"

Emma sighed. "I just wish we were back in Mexico. Things were so much easier there."

"Hmm." Dad began loading dishes into the dishwasher. "Easier how?"

Emma shrugged. "Things just made sense. I didn't have to worry so much about everything."

Dad stopped and looked at her. "What are you worried about?"

*Everything!*

Emma handed him a batch of plates as she began listing off all the things that kept her up at night. "What if I say the wrong thing at school and the kids laugh at me? What if a teacher calls on me and I don't know the answer? What if I walk down the wrong street and I get lost? What if my friends back home forget about me? What if nobody here wants to be my friend?"

This last one was hard to say, and Emma felt tears prickling her eyes.

"Ah, those are big worries." He put the plates

down and went to give Emma a hug. "I'm sorry you're feeling this way," Dad said. "It's really hard when things change."

Emma nodded. "I wish they didn't change," she said, and now she really was crying.

When she pulled back, Dad took her hands and said, "Would you like some advice?"

"Yes, please." She wiped her eyes on her sleeve.

"When we find ourselves in a new and unfamiliar situation, it can feel like things are out of our control."

Emma nodded.

"And some of them are. But not all."

She waited.

"The key is to assess your situation and determine what's in your control and what's not. Then change what you can, to make your situation better. And let go of what you can't control."

It sounded like good advice.

"For example," Dad said. "You're worried that nobody wants to be your friend."

Emma's throat tightened a little bit, and she nodded.

"What can *you* do in that situation? What's in *your* control?"

"I don't know!" Emma sighed. "Nothing."

"Well, that's not true at all. Think of it like a mystery you have to solve."

Instantly, Emma's detective brain clicked into gear.

She thought about what she used to do in Mexico whenever there was a "new kid" in school. Usually, she would go up and talk to them or sit next to them during lunch. She would do what she could to make them feel welcome.

Emma realized she was waiting for someone to do that for her here, but maybe that wasn't going to happen. Maybe *she* had to be the one to go up and talk to someone.

That was certainly in her control.

But also terrifying because what would she even say?

As they finished cleaning up, Emma pondered the question.

By the time they were done, she was nowhere closer to an answer. The rest of the family was set up and waiting for them to watch a movie, so Emma and Dad finished wiping the kitchen counter and joined everyone on the couch.

## The Heron Princess

The next morning, after a breakfast of huevos rancheros, Abuela was sitting on Martín's bed with a heavy leather tome on her lap. Etched on the cover of the book was an image of a pyramid below the words MEXICO LINDO Y QUERIDO.

On the first page was a list of names, all the people in Martín and Emma's family who had owned this book before them. Abuela had been the last, until she had added Martín's and Emma's names when she gave them the book.

"Oh, I remember this legend!" Abuela pointed at a page titled "The Sleeping Princess and the Warrior."

"That was a fiery one," she added.

"Because of the volcanoes?" Martín asked. Two volcanoes, Popocatépetl and Iztaccíhuatl, were drawn on the page.

"Yes," Abuela said. Then she smiled. "And also... it's a love story."

"Gross," Martín replied, quickly turning the pages to the next legend.

As they flipped through the book, he kept his eye out for the conch symbol indicating the legend was unlocked and ready for the Legendarios to visit.

Martín, Emma, and Abuela were all Legendarios, or legend travelers. But they couldn't just go into any legend. The book always chose a specific legend for them to travel into, a story the book's owners needed to hear at that moment in their life. Martín wasn't exactly sure how the book knew which legend to choose. However, once the legend was selected, a small spiral showed up on the top of the title page.

"There!" Emma pointed at the spiral marking on the title page of one of the legends.

"The Heron Princess," Abuela read. "I'm not familiar with this story." She quickly scanned the first few lines and then said, "It's set on Lake Pátzcuaro, in Michoacán. The lake is beautiful, surrounded by volcanic mountains."

Abuela looked up at the twins. "So, what do you say?" she asked. "Shall we go exploring?"

"Definitely!" Martín said.

"Does everyone have their magical token?" Emma asked.

She touched the bracelet on her arm, a thin circle made of metal vines intertwined with real vines. Martín had an identical one on his arm. They were souvenirs from one of their previous Legendarios adventures, when he and Emma explored a legend about the beginning of all things. The bracelets were also magical objects and important for them to be able to get back home. Otherwise, they might be stuck inside a legend until it ended, which could take a lifetime!

Abuela held out her hand, showing them a ring made out of smooth blue stone.

"That's your magical object?" Martín asked. Abuela had worn that ring for as long as Martín had known her.

"It's made of lapis lazuli," Abuela explained. "It was used in a fire ceremony in one of the first legends I visited. The ring stays as cool as ice no matter how much you heat it up."

"Cool!" Martín said.

"Okay, hold Abuela's hand," Emma told him.

Her fingers were wrapped around the black disk of obsidian that she wore on a leather string around her neck. With her other hand, she pressed her finger to the conch symbol on the title page. Instantly, the outline of an archway took shape on the wall, and a soft breeze began to blow through the room.

"Ready?" Emma asked.

Abuela squeezed Martín's hand, and he squeezed back.

"Ready!" Martín said, and they followed Emma through the portal and into a new Legendarios adventure.

## A Mysterious Lake

Emma stepped onto squishy mud.

*Squelch.*

"Ewww." She lifted her mud-covered sneaker.

"Oh dear," said Abuela, walking carefully so as not to slip on the swampy wetlands.

Fat cattails bopped on thin stems among other tall grass and reedy plants. A bright green salamander scurried over Emma's feet, and she yelped.

"Lake Pátzcuaro," Abuela said, spreading her arms wide.

In the center of the lake were six little islands. Narrow canoes drifted on the lake around the islands.

"I've never seen boats like those," Emma said.

Lying across the front of each boat was something that looked like giant butterfly wings made of mesh netting.

"I believe those are fishing nets," Abuela said.

Just then one of the fishermen lifted the object, and a huge net unfurled beneath it. He dipped it into the water, using the gigantic net to scoop out fish!

Emma thought it was very impressive. But not nearly as impressive as what she saw next.

A young woman in a beautiful dress was gliding in one of the canoes toward the fisherman. She had yellow flowers in her braided hair, and her face glowed like sunlight. As she drifted past the fishing boats, fish just leaped out of the water and jumped right into the nets.

"Whoa!" said Martín.

It wasn't just the fish that were behaving strangely. Flocks of different birds circled over her head; lily pads blossomed when they bumped into her boat; even the water in front

of her boat seemed to part, making it easier for her to glide through the lake.

At that moment the young woman spotted Emma, Martín, and Abuela on the shore. She waved, and her canoe veered toward them.

Her boat came to a gentle stop by the shore.

"Hello," the woman said as she stepped out of her boat.

"Hi," said Emma, and she introduced herself, Martín, and Abuela.

"I am Hapunda," the young woman replied. "Welcome to Lake Pátzcuaro."

A squirt of water seemed to jump out of the lake just then and reach toward her; it looked like a rope, and the tip was growing into a bubble. The bubble got bigger and bigger and then ... it popped. Inside it was a yellow water lily.

Abuela laughed, and Hapunda handed her the flower.

"Thank you," Abuela said, and tucked it behind her ear.

"What brings you to our beautiful lake?" Hapunda asked.

"We're looking for a princ—" Martín blurted out.

But Emma elbowed him. "We heard it's a very special place," she said.

"Indeed it is!" The young woman laughed.

Behind Hapunda, the lake stilled completely, turning into what looked like a mirror, perfectly reflecting each little boat with its butterfly nets, every detail of every branch bending over the water, each bird flying overhead.

Then, as suddenly as it began, the effect ended and the lake went back to being a normal lake. Little waves pushed up against Hapunda's legs.

"Oh, now, that was quite something," said Abuela.

"Did you do that?" Emma asked Hapunda.

"Lake Pátzcuaro did that," Hapunda explained. "Pátzcuaro is my friend. More than my friend, actually. My beloved."

"What?" Martín said, practically choking on the word. "That doesn't make sense."

And Emma agreed. But also, the lake seemed to wrap itself around Hapunda's legs, like the water was trying to give her a hug.

"Would you like to hear the story of Lake Pátzcuaro?" Hapunda asked.

"It sounds like it's going to be a love story," Martín groaned.

"It is," Hapunda replied. "But not the kind you expect."

Emma loved mysteries, and this lake was definitely behaving in a mysterious way.

"Sure," she replied, ignoring how Martín scowled at her.

"Perhaps you would help me gather some

of the fruits I've come here to collect, and I can tell you the story as we take the harvest back to my island?"

"We have to work *and* hear a love story?" Martín grumbled. That made Abuela chuckle.

"We'd be happy to help," Abuela replied.

"Thank you." Hapunda grabbed some baskets from her canoe.

She handed one to Emma and one to Martín.

She then turned to Abuela. "It'll be a bit uneven and muddy where we're going. Perhaps you prefer to stay here and admire the view?"

A squirt of water suddenly leaped out of the lake in an arch. A second squirt arched next to it and then a third. The three arches danced before Abuela, going high and low, fat and skinny, even twirling around like swirls.

"Pátzcuaro loves to entertain," Hapunda added.

"And I will be a willing audience," Abuela replied. She found a seat on a smooth stone by the shore.

"See you soon," Emma told Abuela, and they followed Hapunda into the trees.

## The Power of Pátzcuaro

Martín had no idea where they were going, but Hapunda definitely seemed to know her way around.

"This area," Hapunda explained, "has rich earth that grows a lot of delicious fruits and vegetables." She pointed out a tree with a cluster of dark green drop-like fruits hanging heavily from the branches.

"Are those avocados?" Martín asked.

"Indeed, they are," Hapunda replied.

"I love avocados!" said Martín. "And what are those?"

The small orange fruit looked like a plum.

"Those are nísperos," Hapunda explained.

"I know those are guavas," Emma said, pointing at a pink-orange fruit. Guavas were her favorite.

Hapunda nodded.

Now that he was paying attention, Martín realized the jungle was bursting with food everywhere he looked.

"These"—Hapunda grabbed a branch packed with fruits that looked like Ping-Pong balls in colors from light green to bright red; she turned to Martín—"are jocotes."

Martín had never seen this fruit before.

"Try one," Hapunda said.

As soon as Martín bit into it, his taste buds

began to tingle. It was not a flavor he had expected, a combination of mango and apple that was sweet and sour all in one.

"These are delicious!" Emma said, wiping her mouth. "They might be my new favorite."

The next fruit they harvested was not a favorite. Nanches tasted like a mix of banana and pear and stinky cheese! Yuck.

The last thing they harvested were chayotes, which Martín knew and loved, so that was okay.

With their baskets full, they made their way back to Abuela. Martín noticed that the plants would all move aside on their own to make room for them. It reminded him of the silly aluxes in one of their earlier legends and how they could bend the jungle to their will.

But with Hapunda, it wasn't just the plants. Birds would stop midflight and dance in front of Hapunda. A trio of frogs kept leaping from branch to branch alongside them. Snakes and turtles joined the procession. The turtles were moving too slowly to keep up, but Martín was certain they were at least trying.

"The animals are being strange, right?" Martín whispered to Emma.

"Totally," she said.

"All of this is Pátzcuaro's doing," Hapunda explained.

"The lake?" Martín asked, but just then the lake answered the question.

Martín spotted Abuela laughing and clapping where she sat on her rock looking out over the lake. And the lake was doing things Martín had never seen water do before: tall waves were forming right at the shore, rising high up like a wall but never crashing! The waves were like never-ending waterfalls, and little fish were jumping in and out of the falling water.

"That's incredible!" Martín said.

"It's impossible," Emma whispered, though they had been on enough adventures to know that a lot of unexpected things were actually possible.

"So how does the lake do that?" Martín asked.

"That," Hapunda replied, "is the story I will tell you on the way to Yunuen."

The lake nudged Hapunda's canoe onto the shores, and she loaded up the three baskets. Martín and Emma helped Abuela onto the boat, and then they all climbed in after her. While they were getting on, the boat didn't wobble once. It was almost as if the lake had become solid, holding the boat tightly in place. It even looked solid, like it was made of stone. But as soon as they were all seated, the boat began bobbing gently.

"Thank you for your help with the harvest," Hapunda told Martín and Emma. "And now I owe you a story."

They sat back, ready to listen.

"My story starts with a star...."

## The Love Story

Hapunda was definitely glowing as she began her story. Emma realized it was because the lake was reflecting rays of sunlight onto Hapunda's face.

"Lake Pátzcuaro wasn't always here," Hapunda explained. "A long, long time ago, it was all trees here. As far as the eye could see."

"What happened?" Emma asked.

"A bright and beautiful star plummeted

from the sky," Hapunda replied. When she said this, little squirts of water began to jump around the canoe.

Hapunda continued with her story. "The star was cast away by Curicaueri, the sun god, who envied the star's beauty and sent it to the earth as punishment. Of course, you can imagine what happened when the star crashed."

"It probably created a huge crater," Martín replied.

Hapunda nodded. "In fact, the crater was so big that it made a crack in the earth, all the way to an underground river. Eventually, the river flooded into the crater, forming a lake." She extended her arms wide. "*This* lake."

"Oh..." Martín's jaw dropped.

"And Pátzcuaro was the castaway star," Hapunda added.

"So the lake is named after the star?" Emma asked.

Hapunda smiled. "Well, it's more like the lake *is* the star."

"What?" Emma leaned over one side of the boat, and her brother leaned over the other.

They dipped their fingers into the water. "You mean I'm touching a star?" Emma asked.

"Yes," Hapunda said, gazing over the edge. Her face was reflected in the water perfectly.

"Although, more precisely," she said, "the star and the water melded into each other and became one, Lake Pátzcuaro."

A tendril of water rose out of the lake and touched Hapunda's face. She smiled.

"You have fallen in love with the star," Abuela said.

"That's weird," Martín mumbled.

"And the star loves you back," Abuela added.

Hapunda nodded.

"That's even weirder," Martín said.

Emma had heard a lot of strange love

stories, but she had to agree, this was the oddest of them all.

A million questions ran through her mind. However, they were fast approaching Hapunda's island, and Emma could see a bunch of men and women and children on the shore waving their arms at Hapunda.

"Welcome to Yunuen," Hapunda said.

But the people weren't smiling as they rushed over to help pull the canoe onto the shore.

"Princess Hapunda," one person began. "You must hurry home."

"Princess?" Emma said. She and Martín looked at each other.

Hapunda frowned. "Why? What's wrong?"

One of the fishermen explained, "We've received word that an enemy tribe of warriors is making their way toward Lake Pátzcuaro."

"Oh no!" Hapunda cried.

"Your father gathered his council," the fisherman told her. "Your brothers went out this morning to see if they could get more information."

Hapunda thanked the fisherman, then turned to Emma, Martín, and Abuela.

"I'm sorry," she said. "This is not how I had hoped to welcome you to our island."

"It's okay." Abuela put her hand on

Hapunda's shoulder. "Sometimes things are out of our hands. Like a boat in the water"—she pointed at the lake—"we need to go where the currents of fate take us."

Hapunda nodded. "Yes, you're right."

She bade them all to follow her, and the four of them raced through the village to Hapunda's house.

As soon as Emma saw it, though, she thought that calling it a "house" was not quite accurate. It was a palace!

"This is your home?" she asked Hapunda as they approached a large pyramid and began climbing the stairs.

"Yes," Hapunda replied, looking over her shoulder at Emma, who was helping Abuela up the steep climb. "I'm sorry there are so many stairs."

"It's all right. You go on," Abuela told her, and Hapunda raced to the top.

Once there, Hapunda went to a group of guards and pointed at Emma, Martín, and Abuela. The guards ran down to meet them. Two guards picked up Abuela and began carrying her up the stairs. Another guard reached for Emma.

"I'm okay," Emma said. "I can walk on my own." She followed behind Abuela.

"I'll take the help," Martín replied, and happily jumped into the arms of one of the guards, who swiftly carried him up the rest of the way.

At the top, Hapunda was waiting in front of a stone temple.

"Welcome to my home," she said. She smiled, but Emma could tell Hapunda was nervous.

The guards set Abuela down.

"Thank you so much," Abuela said, and the guards nodded before flanking Hapunda.

"Please, follow me," Hapunda instructed.

## Danger Approaches

Martín followed Hapunda and her guards inside a temple at the top of the pyramid. There were a lot of people gathered in little groups, and everyone seemed worried.

Martín stood on one side of Abuela, and Emma stood on the other.

"Hapunda!" an old man called out.

"Father," Hapunda replied, and she ran to

him. Martín, Emma, and Abuela stayed where they were.

"Father?" Martín whispered. "He looks like her grandfather."

"That he does." Abuela chuckled.

Just then there was a commotion behind them, and everyone turned to look at the entrance.

Martín turned as well and saw four young men at the entrance to the palace. They were all different heights, but they all stood tall and strong.

"My sons!" the old man called. "What have you learned?"

The four men walked through the crowd toward the king. Everyone fell silent.

"They're coming for *her*!" one of the brothers said, and he pointed at Hapunda.

The crowd gasped. "The princess!"

"No!" someone cried.

"That's impossible," said another voice.

"Not Hapunda!"

"Why me?" Hapunda's voice was quiet, but everyone heard her.

"Word has spread of your beauty," one of her brothers replied.

"Your kindness," another brother added.

"Your wisdom," the third brother said.

"They want you to marry their chief," said the fourth brother.

"Ewww," said Martín.

One of Hapunda's brothers explained. "The chief's wife died, and he is looking for a new bride. He wants to marry a princess."

"Absolutely not!" the king cried.

"We will fight them!" someone in the crowd called out.

"We can't," one of the brothers replied. "Their tribe numbers in the hundreds!"

"That's a lot of people," Martín whispered.

The crowd began to huddle around Hapunda.

"You have been so good to us!"

"We won't let them take you."

"We will do anything to help you!"

The voices were getting louder.

"Oh dear," said Abuela.

"What if we hide her in the palace?" one of the brothers suggested.

"I'm sure they'll search every part of it until they find her," the king replied.

"We can escape with her to the next village," another brother said.

"And live in exile?" Hapunda asked. "Besides, when they don't find me here, that's where they'll go next. And then I will just have to run away once more. I can't keep running forever!"

"But it would buy us some time to come up with a better plan," the king replied.

It was a good point, and everyone wanted to share their opinion. They all started speaking at once. Some people were even crying. But Hapunda smiled, and her face seemed calm. "Friends, give me time. I will find another way."

"How?" someone cried.

"What way?" said another.

"Your brothers said they'll be here by tomorrow!"

Abuela sighed. "This is not a good situation for Hapunda."

Martín turned to her and saw that Abuela looked tired. He realized this had probably been a lot more adventure than she had been through in a long time.

"Do you want to sit down?" he asked her.

"Oh, yes, actually. That would be lovely."

Martín and Emma led Abuela out of the throne room and to a ledge where they could sit with their backs against the palace, looking out at the lake.

"It's so pretty here, isn't it?" Emma asked. "The lake looks like a pool made of sky trapped between the mountains."

Martín thought that was very poetic and also true.

From the top of the temple, they could see the other islands near Yunuen and lots of little boats fishing between the islands.

"What's that?" Emma asked, pointing at a curl of smoke rising from the shoreline in the distance.

"That's probably the enemy tribe," Martín said.

"They do look pretty close," Emma replied.

"Too close," Abuela added.

At that moment Hapunda came out to join

them. She was followed by one of her brothers.

"I only ask for this evening to think," she told him. "If I don't come up with a better plan by tomorrow morning, then I will let you take me to the next village."

Her brother nodded and then walked back into the palace, where Martín could still hear many anxious voices. Hapunda's name was said again and again.

She sighed and joined them on the ledge.

"They're worried about you," Abuela told Hapunda.

"I know," she replied.

"What will you do?" Emma asked.

Hapunda looked up. "What I always do when I'm in a bind. Come, let's go talk to Pátzcuaro."

## The Right-Size Bubble

Emma wasn't sure she heard Hapunda correctly.

"Did you say talk to Pátzcuaro?"

"Yes." Hapunda was on her feet and leading them back to the stairs. They looked awfully steep from the very top, and there were so many.

Emma looked over at Abuela walking slowly toward her with Martín.

"Ummm... do you think you'll be able to go down?" Emma asked Abuela.

"Yes," Abuela replied. "But very slowly and very carefully."

They began their descent, step by slow and careful step. Hapunda tried to hide it, but it was clear she was anxious to get down quickly.

Abuela must have picked up on that as well because she stopped and said, "Why don't you two go on ahead? Martín can help me down the rest of the way. Right, Martín?"

Martín nodded.

"Are you sure?" Hapunda replied. "I don't mind waiting."

"I'm sure," Abuela said. "Now go on. We'll wait for you at the bottom."

"Thank you," Hapunda said, and she began descending more quickly. Emma tried to keep up, moving quickly but also carefully so as not to slip. It reminded her of trying to avoid sliding down Mount Tlaloc in the rain when they had gone on their first Legendario adventure.

They soon reached the bottom, and Emma turned to wave at Abuela and Martín. Her brother waved back, and Abuela urged them onward.

"See you soon!" Emma called, and then took off running after Hapunda.

They raced through the trees toward the shore. As they approached, Emma noticed what looked like a green tunnel made of leaves, vines, and branches.

As soon as Emma and Hapunda stepped into the tunnel, flowers began sprouting directly over Hapunda's head, on the branches beside them, and even on the ground around her feet!

With every step Hapunda took, the flowers vanished and then reappeared wherever she stood.

"What . . . ? How . . . ?" Emma couldn't even

find the words to ask what was going on.

"It's Pátzcuaro," Hapunda explained. "Hurry," she added.

They didn't stop running until they reached the end of the tunnel, where the ground went from being soft moss to soft sand. Hapunda suddenly came to a halt, and Emma bumped into her, falling back on her bum.

"Are you okay?" Hapunda asked, extending her hand to help Emma up.

"Yes, thanks." Emma rose and wiped sand off her pants, but she was unable to take her eyes off the sight in front of her.

A huge glass mirror stood upright on the surface of the water. In it, Emma could see her reflection perfectly, standing right next to Hapunda. Then the mirror became a clear circle of glass, like a window. Except it wasn't glass—it was water—and in that circle stood a person. He was a little taller than Hapunda, with black hair tied back in a ponytail. His skin was golden brown, and he was glowing. Like a star.

*A star!* Emma thought.

"Is that...?" She turned to Hapunda, who wore the biggest smile Emma had ever seen.

"My beloved," Hapunda replied. "Emma, this is Pátzcuaro. Pátzcuaro, meet Emma."

The young man bowed.

Hapunda turned to Emma and in a very serious voice said, "Nobody can know about this. You must promise not to tell anyone about what you have seen."

"Why?" Emma asked. "It's amazing!"

"My father, my brothers..." Hapunda shook her head. "They wouldn't understand. They only think in terms of war. They would think it's an enchantment from an enemy tribe, put here to lure me into a trap.

"If they ever found out about us"—Hapunda

turned to look at Pátzcuaro—"they would forbid me from ever coming back here."

Pátzcuaro's face sank with sadness.

"I won't say anything. I promise." Emma put her hand on her heart.

Pátzcuaro spoke then. "My darling, would you like to go for a boat ride?"

Emma was glad Martín had stayed behind with Abuela. She knew he would probably be rolling his eyes right now and saying things like "ewww" and "gross."

Pátzcuaro moved his hand, and a boat made of water appeared next to him. The boat rippled and shimmered in the light, but it also looked as solid as if it were made of wood.

"Oh, Pátzcuaro!" Hapunda cried, shaking her head. "I'm afraid I have terrible news."

She explained what they had learned earlier. "And the enemy tribe will be here by tomorrow evening!"

Emma was surprised to see how distraught the princess was. She had seemed so calm and untroubled when she was talking to the king and her brothers.

"My father and brothers want to take me to the next village," Hapunda went on, "but I can't just keep running from one place to another. I have to solve this problem here."

Pátzcuaro nodded. "I agree, fleeing won't work. And besides, I would miss you terribly."

"So, what am I to do?" Hapunda began crying.

She looked up at Pátzcuaro. "If only I could hide with you."

Something in Emma's brain clicked, the familiar wheels of her detective brain kicking into motion. If Hapunda could hide in the lake somehow, the enemy tribe would have to leave when they failed to find her. And even if they went to the next village and the next, they'd never find her. It was the perfect solution!

But how to make it work?

Enma thought about when they first met Hapunda by the shore. How a bubble that hid a yellow water lily had risen out of the water. She remembered how the water around their boat had turned solid, as if it were made of stone. And she had just seen a mirror made of water, reflecting their surroundings perfectly.

"That's it!" Emma said. "Pátzcuaro, do you remember the bubble you made that had the flower inside it?"

"You mean like this?" A long vine reached out of the water with a bubble attached to the end.

"Yes! How big can you make it?"

Hapunda turned to Emma. "What are you thinking?"

"I'm thinking that maybe you *can* hide with Pátzcuaro. In the lake! If he makes a bubble that's big enough for you to fit in..."

"I can!" Pátzcuaro replied, and the bubble grew and grew.

"And then maybe you can make it solid so Hapunda can stand in it. And reflective," Emma went on. "Like a mirror. That way it will reflect the surroundings—"

"So nobody will be able to see it!" Hapunda replied. "Emma, that's genius!"

In less than three seconds, Pátzcuaro had built a perfectly reflective bubble that was just the right size for Hapunda.

"My lady," he said, and the side of the bubble opened up. A watery path extended from the bubble to the shore. Emma could see the inside of the bubble was laid out like a room, with a table and chairs and even a sparkly chandelier hanging from the ceiling.

"Let's go take a look," Hapunda said, taking Emma by the hand and stepping onto the watery carpet.

## Trapped!

It had been slow going, but finally Abuela and Martín reached the last step.

"Oof!" Abuela said. She took a deep breath. "I think this may very well be my last adventure."

"What?" Martín's eyes got wide and filled with tears a lot more quickly than he expected. "Are you dying?"

Abuela laughed and pulled Martín into

a hug. "No, silly. I just mean that I'm getting a little too old for Legendarios adventures. It takes a lot out of an old lady like me to be traipsing around the forest, running up and down a million stairs, and living through such dramatic turns of events."

They walked over to a tree stump so Abuela could sit down.

"Though I suppose that's exactly what makes for a good legend," Abuela went on as she sat on the stump.

Martín sat on the ground beside her.

"Do you like being a Legendario?" she asked him.

"I love it!" Martín told her. "There's always a great adventure and some kind of magic, and you get to meet some pretty interesting people. Though some of the legends are a bit scary."

Abuela nodded. "Not unlike life."

At that moment two things happened at

the same time. First, Martín spotted Emma running toward them from the right. Hapunda was not with her.

Second, voices began yelling from the top of the temple, and Hapunda's brothers started running down the stairs.

"Martín." Emma stopped in front of him. In between breaths, she explained her plan for hiding Hapunda in a bubble.

By the time she finished, Hapunda's brothers had descended the temple and ran toward Martín, Abuela, and Emma.

"Shhh," Emma whispered to Martín. "Don't say anything to her brothers."

"Where is Hapunda?" they asked a moment later.

It was obvious they were angry about something, so Martín asked, "What's wrong?"

But the brothers ignored him. "Where is our sister?" they demanded.

"She's hiding," Emma replied.

"Hiding? Where? Did she go to the next village?"

"No," Emma said. "But . . . I can't tell you where she is."

That made the brothers even more angry. All four of them were scowling.

"What have you done to her?" one of the brothers asked.

"Nothing, I promise. You just have to trust me."

"Trust you?" one of the brothers asked. "We just met you! How do we know you're not working with the enemy tribe?"

"That's right," said another. "Maybe you've taken our sister and handed her over already."

"I wouldn't do that!" Emma cried back.

"Besides," Martín added, "you saw us arrive with her."

"That proves nothing." One brother grabbed Emma's arm, and she winced.

"Hey." Martín got to his feet. "Let go of my sister."

Another brother grabbed his arm and squeezed tightly. "Ouch. Let me go!" Martín shouted.

"Not until you tell us where Hapunda is."

"I can't tell you," Emma said again. "I'm sorry.

I promised her I wouldn't say anything."

"I don't believe you!" one of the brothers replied. Then he said, "Lock them up!"

They began dragging Emma and Martín away.

"Oh, please wait," Abuela said. "Surely you don't need to resort to such drastic measures."

The brothers responded by grabbing Abuela, though more gently than how they were gripping Martín and Emma.

"Let's go," they said.

"You don't understand," Emma was saying. "Hapunda made me promise not to tell anyone where she was hiding!"

Martín, Emma, and Abuela were taken to a clearing with many small structures. The structures were made of stone on all four sides, with a heavy door in the front. They seemed barely big enough to fit one person.

"Let me go!" Martín yelled, and he was suddenly released. But only long enough to be shoved into one of the stone enclosures. The heavy wooden door slammed shut.

Martín immediately began pushing on the door, to no avail. It was closed tightly.

Small slits were carved into the stone, letting in slabs of slanted light and, fortunately, clean air because...

"Ugh. Gross! What is that smell?" Martín gagged.

The floor looked, smelled, and felt like it had never been cleaned. It was sticky in some parts, slimy in others. Martín thought it had once upon a time been covered by straw, but now that straw was totally caked to the floor.

Plus other things too.

"Emma!" Martín yelled.

Distantly, he heard his sister's voice. "I'm over here!"

Martín peered through the slits, but it

was impossible to tell which stone prison was Emma's and where Abuela was.

"Are you okay?" he asked.

"Yes!"

"Abuela?" he asked.

"I'm fine," Abuela replied.

It was good that everyone was fine, but...

"What are we going to do?" he called out as Emma voiced the same question.

## A Plan Interrupted

Emma knew they wouldn't spend forever trapped in the stone prisons. Eventually the legend would end and they would automatically return to Chicago. But Abuela had told them that legends could last a long time, even years in some cases.

They did not have years to wait for that to happen.

Besides, based on the shouting Emma could hear outside, it was clear that things were getting worse.

If they were together, she would have activated the necklace and pulled them out of the legend so they could go back home. If they wanted to, they could always go back into the legend after that and maybe do things a little differently, like maybe not get trapped.

But they weren't together, which meant that if Emma activated the necklace, she would be the only one to return. Martín and Abuela would stay behind, stuck in this legend until Emma was able to come back for them. And she had a lot of concerns about that.

It seemed Abuela was thinking the same thing because she suddenly called out, "Emma? You have your necklace?"

"Yes."

"I was thinking, what if you go back—"

"I won't leave you stranded here," Emma quickly replied.

"I would hope not." Abuela laughed, and it made Emma feel a little bit better to know that Abuela wasn't too scared.

"What I was thinking," Abuela continued, "was that perhaps you could go back and then return to the legend at a different point. A bit later on in the story."

"That's a great idea!" Martín's voice was coming from a place farther away than Abuela's. Emma peered through the slits in the stone prison, but she couldn't really tell where he was.

It was a good idea, and Emma knew how to do it. She and Martín had actually done that very thing in a prior legend. But that time they had been together, both of them traveling out of the book and back into it at the same time.

This was very different.

And now that Emma's problem-solving mind was in full gear, she could think of a hundred things that could go wrong under these different circumstances.

"Abuela, did you ever try doing something like this?" Emma asked.

"No. I always traveled alone," came the reply.

"What if I can't come back?" Emma asked.

"Why would that happen?" Martín asked in return.

"Well, maybe the legend thinks we got what we needed out of the story and it locks up and then I can't activate it."

"Oh. I didn't think of that," her brother said.

"I wouldn't worry," Abuela chimed in. "I don't think this story is quite done with us yet."

Emma sort of agreed. After all, they usually had to complete some task or learn something important before the legend closed up, and so far none of that had happened.

"Well," Emma continued with her concerns, "what if I do come back but in a different part of the lake and then I can't find you?"

She knew that was unlikely though. The legend was what it was, and the story usually followed the same path every time. The story had led them here, to these stone prisons, and that was where it would lead her every time.

But Emma had other concerns. "What if I come back and I get captured before I can rescue you? Or what if I get lost finding my way here? We were with Hapunda the last time. Or what if I—"

"My dear Emma," Abuela interrupted. "You are a bright and very capable girl. I have absolutely no doubt that you will reach us and be able to get us out of here."

"Me too!" Martín called out.

It felt good to know they trusted her.

"Now go," Abuela added. "It sounds like

things are getting a bit heated out there."

Abuela was referring to the raised voices and shouts coming from various people Emma could see running by outside their prisons.

"The enemy tribe has been spotted at the shore," someone cried. "They'll be here in no time."

People frantically rushed to pick up spears and anything they could use to defend themselves.

"Emma?" Martín asked. "Did you leave yet?"

"No. I'm still here."

"Why?" her brother asked. "You should hurry!"

"Okay." Emma nodded. "I'll be right back."

She wrapped her hand around the obsidian necklace and then placed her finger on the delicate bracelet around her wrist. Immediately, the portal opened and her bedroom appeared on the stone wall.

She stepped through, and with a slurping

sound, the portal closed behind her. Emma found herself standing in the calm quiet of her room. She allowed herself one breath before rushing for the book of legends.

"Pencil... pencil... pencil." She searched the room frantically, finding a pencil tucked into her math workbook on her desk. Emma opened the book to the legend of Hapunda and Pátzcuaro. She began skimming the pages of the book.

"We did that...

"We saw that...

"We met Hapunda..."

Emma moved her finger down the page, reading as quickly as she could, trying to find a good place to reenter. Once she found that, all she had to do was draw a spiral with her pencil, and she could open up a portal in that part of the legend.

*KNOCK, KNOCK.*

"There you are." Mami poked her head in. "I was looking for you." Mami eyed the room. "Where's Martín?"

"Oh ... ummm ... he ..."

Mami frowned. "Is everything okay?"

"Yeah. No. It's just that ... well ..."

Her mind was spinning, and her words were all jumbled up. She was mumbling nonsense, and that made Mami frown even more.

"Oh, wait a minute," Mami said. "Is today the day he was going to meet up with his friend to work on their project?"

"Yes! Yes, today is that day," Emma replied, her voice a tight squeak.

She knew she sounded weird, but Mami didn't seem to notice.

"And I guess Abuela went for a walk. She's not downstairs."

"Yeah, probably." Emma bit her lip as she thought about Abuela trapped in a stone prison inside a centuries-old legend. With enemies fast approaching.

"So...," Emma began, "did you need something?"

"Actually, yes," Mami said. "I need you to come with me to pick up the cake for tonight."

"What! Now?"

Mami nodded. "I lost track of time, and the shop is closing in thirty minutes."

Emma glanced over at the book. "I'm sort of in the middle of something," she said.

Mami glanced over at the book as well. "You can bring it if you want. It's just hard for me to find parking near the shop, so I need you to run in and pick up the cake for me while I wait in the car."

"That's not going to work," Emma replied.

"What's not going to work?"

"I mean . . ." Emma swallowed. "I can't bring the book with me. Can't someone else go with you?" Emma was starting to get frantic.

"Well, I'd ask Martín or Abuela, but . . ." Mami glanced around the room again.

*They're trapped in stone prisons.*

"Fine." Emma stood up quickly. "But let's hurry."

## Some Handy Wizardry

Martín knew Emma had left because he saw rays of light shooting out of one of the stone prisons. The guards noticed the light too, and they immediately ran to see what was happening.

"Open the door!" one of the guards instructed, and his companion unlocked the door and yanked it open.

"What is the meaning of this?" the first guard asked. "Where is the girl?"

The other guard looked just as confused. He shrugged.

"A person cannot just disappear like that," the first guard yelled. "People don't just vanish!"

"Of course not!" the second guard agreed.

"So what happened?"

By then a group had gathered around the stone prison. Martín couldn't pick up everything they were saying because at the same time there were shouts and cries of alarm coming from the pyramid and the lake. He did manage to hear one word, and then everyone turned to look at him.

"Magos."

"They think we're wizards!" Martín whispered under his breath.

A moment later his door was yanked open, and light flooded in. He blinked as his eyes tried to adjust to the light. Two large guards reached in and grabbed him, pulling him out. Abuela was also being taken out of her prison, though more gently.

"Where did the other one go?" the guards asked Martín. "How did she vanish?"

There was nothing preventing Martín from explaining about the book of legends and being a Legendario. But he knew the guards wouldn't understand or even believe him. Although, apparently, they did believe in magic.

So that's what he said. "It was magic."

The guards' eyes went wide, and some of them began nodding.

"You are magos, then?" a guard asked.

"In a way," Martín replied. He looked over at Abuela, and she nodded in agreement.

"Then you will help us defeat the enemy." The guards didn't even let Martín respond before they led him and Abuela back to the big temple, where Hapunda's father and brothers were holding court.

Martín gulped. What exactly did they think *he* could do?

The guards carried Abuela up the stairs, and Martín followed behind them. One of Hapunda's brothers met them at the top.

"Why are these prisoners free?" he demanded.

"They are magos," said the guard holding Martín.

"Are they, now?" the brother replied. "Well, that certainly changes things."

Martín and Abuela were taken to Hapunda's father.

"I welcomed you into my kingdom, and you thank me by taking away my daughter," the king yelled.

"No, that's not what happened," Martín replied.

"She went into hiding on her own," Abuela explained.

"And you know where she is?" the king asked.

"Yes," Abuela replied. "But we cannot tell you."

"Why should I believe you?"

"Because we are on your side," Martín replied. "We want to help you and Hapunda."

The king nodded. "Very well, then. You claim to be magos. That will certainly turn the tides in our favor. What can you do?"

"Ummm..." Martín glanced over at Abuela. "Maybe those would be useful."

He pointed at her earlobes. Abuela took off one of the clip-on party favor earrings that Martín had given her and held it out in the palm of her hand.

"You push it here." She pressed down in the center of the earring and it lit up a bright pink.

The guards around her gasped and took a step back.

"What wizardry is this!" the king exclaimed. He pinched the earring between his thumb and forefinger.

Martín tried not to giggle.

"Oh!" Martín then added, "I also have this."

He reached into his pocket and pulled out the sticky hand he'd gotten as a party favor. It was coated in lint and a scrap of paper, which Martín peeled off.

The king eyed him skeptically.

"Watch." Martín slipped his finger into the small loop on one end and flung the sticky hand out. With a slurp, it attached to one of the guards.

"Unhand me!" the guard cried, moving away, but the sticky hand

only stretched farther, stuck fast to the guard's arm.

"Now, *that* is powerful sorcery!" the king said, and he walked over to Martín. "How does it work?"

Martín detached the sticky hand from the startled guard, who rubbed at his arm vigorously.

Martín slipped his finger out of the sticky loop and passed it over to the king. He explained how to fling it, and the king hurled the sticky hand across the room.

It smacked one of Hapunda's brothers, who yelped, startled, before the hand retracted and the king caught it deftly.

"I will keep this," the king said.

"That's fine," Martín replied. "Consider it a thank-you gift for letting us go."

"Let you go?" the king said. "That's not possible. Not until we have defeated the enemy tribe."

He flung the hand out once more. This time the guards and Hapunda's brothers were paying attention, and they all stepped out of reach of the neon yellow hand.

"Look!" A shout came from the entrance to the temple. Martín joined the others as they ran to the entrance. A guard was pointing at the lake where the enemy tribe was trying to launch their boats from a distant shore.

Trying and failing.

Every time the enemy warriors loaded up one of their boats and climbed aboard, a huge wave would topple them over. Just as quickly as it arrived, the wave would vanish.

"Is this more of your magic?" the king asked.

"Uh-huh," Martín replied, knowing full well it was Pátzcuaro's doing.

"You really are powerful," the king told him.

Eventually, however, a few of the boats were managing to steady themselves and push away from the opposite shore. Despite the turbulent waters, they kept their boats afloat and were making their way to Yunuen.

Guards and villagers ready to defend their homes were rushing to the beach where the enemy boats were headed.

The king called to one of his guards, a huge man with a serious face. The king gave the sticky hand to this guard. "I entrust this magical token to you. Use it wisely."

The guard accepted the yellow hand with an even more serious expression than before.

"You honor me," he said, and then bowed before accepting the sticky hand. He grimaced briefly while he wrapped the loop around his finger but then turned and made his way down to the beach.

"Let us hope this is enough," the king said.

Martín didn't know whether to laugh or cry as a dozen boats began to make their way to the island.

## Tick, Tick, Tick

Emma was in the car with her seat belt on before Mami had even come out of the house.

"Wow, that must be a really good story," Mami teased as she got into the car.

"Yep. And it's in a really dangerous part." Emma bounced her legs.

*Tick, tick, tick.*

She could almost hear the seconds ticking

past while Abuela and Martín waited for her to come back.

"What's it about?" Mami asked as she pulled out onto the street. But before Emma could respond, Mami was rolling down her window to say hi to their neighbor, Mrs. Grundi.

Mrs. Grundi was the oldest person Emma had ever known. She lived alone with her little dog (which was the oldest dog Emma had ever seen), and when the two of them went out for a walk, it usually took them a half hour just to walk to the end of the block.

"How are you, dear?" Mrs. Grundi asked.

"We're well," Mami replied. "And you?"

*Tick, tick, tick.*

It took all of Emma's willpower to not say anything while Mrs. Grundi told Mami all about her recent doctor's appointment and how her grandkids were doing. When they started trying to forecast the weather for the week, Emma thought she was going to lose it.

"Can I go back inside?" she asked Mami in a whisper.

Mami shook her head, but she also finished her conversation with Mrs. Grundi. Before they pulled away, Mrs. Grundi gave them each a butterscotch candy, which she always carried in her little purse.

"Can't you go faster?" Emma asked as she popped the candy into her mouth. Mami seemed to be driving at a turtle's pace, and they had already wasted ten minutes chatting with Mrs. Grundi.

"This is the speed limit, Emma. I'm not going to put *us* in danger. We're not characters in your story."

Which only made Emma even more nervous.

*Tick, tick, tick.*

After what seemed like hours, Emma could finally see the cake shop at the end of the street. She was out of the car before Mami had even fully stopped.

"Emma!" Mami scolded, but Emma just ran straight to the shop. She yanked open the door, and the little bell above the door jingled happily.

Three people were in line, and even though the first person already had his cake in a box and ready to go, he was still there chatting and laughing with the cashier.

Emma cleared her throat, hoping that would get the cashier's attention. It didn't.

She faked a sneeze.

"Bless you," the person in line ahead of her said.

"Thanks," Emma replied.

*Tick, tick, tick.*

She was bouncing from foot to foot, thinking of all the terrible things that might be happening in Hapunda's village right at *that very moment*. How could everyone just stand here so patiently waiting for cakes when disaster was imminent at any second? Emma felt like she was going to scream.

"Agh!" she groaned. This got the cashier's attention, and she gave Emma a small frown. But it seemed to work. The first person in line thanked the cashier and waved goodbye.

The second and third people did not delay. They got their cakes, paid for them, and left.

"Sorry about the wait," the cashier said when Emma approached.

"It's okay." Emma blushed. She knew she had been rude, even though she hadn't actually meant to groan so loudly.

"I'm here to pick up a cake." Emma gave the cashier her last name, and the cashier brought out the cake. She tied a ribbon around the box, knotting it twice and then making a bow.

*Tick, tick, tick.*

Emma held her breath to keep from groaning at how long everything seemed to be taking.

Then the cashier rang her up. "Oh," she said. "It looks like we're out of paper. Give me a moment."

This time Emma bit her lip to keep herself from crying out as the cashier replaced the roll of paper in the register and rang her up again.

"There we go." She took Emma's money and gave her back the change. "How is your mom?" she asked as Emma grabbed the cake box.

"She's fine. Thanks!" Emma said, and she ran out the door as fast as she could.

Mami was in the street with her blinkers on.

"Let's go," Emma said as soon as she got back into the car.

"Not until you put your seat belt on."

"AGH!" Emma zipped the seat belt across her chest and snapped it in.

*Tick, tick, tick.*

"Emma! What is wrong with you today?"

Emma forced herself to take a deep breath. "I'm sorry," she said in as calm a voice as she

could get. "Do you mind if we go home now? I'm really eager to get back into my story."

Mami shook her head, but she pressed on the gas and drove them home. Even though Mami didn't say anything else on the ride home, Emma could tell Mami was driving as fast as she was allowed to go.

"Thanks!" Emma said as soon as they pulled

up to the house. She waited for Mami to turn off the car and then jumped out, racing up to the door and running in. She was up the stairs, back in her room, and with pencil in hand before Mami even closed the front door.

"Here," Emma said, spotting the perfect place to reenter the legend. It would put her right where she needed to be.

She drew a spiral onto the page. It began to glow. Emma touched her fingertip to the glowing spiral and wrapped her hand around her necklace. Instantly, the portal appeared. Emma didn't waste another minute before she stepped through.

Emma was back on the shore where she had first met Hapunda. Off to the right she could see the enemy tribe battling the lake as they tried to climb onto their boats. Many had already succeeded and were headed to Hapunda's island with torches lit.

"Oh no." Emma sighed. "I need to hurry."

She looked around for a boat but saw none. Which didn't entirely surprise her.

"Okay, think, think, think." She scanned the area for something—anything!—she could use to float on. Her eyes fell on a large piece of driftwood bumping gently against the shore. It was large enough for her to lie on and seemed sturdy enough to hold her entire weight.

Emma pushed it out into the water and carefully slid onto it. Using her arms, she began to paddle across the lake toward Yunuen. The wood glided easily, but her arms were quickly getting tired.

"Just a bit longer," she said to herself, forcing her arms to keep working. Eventually, however, a cramp in her shoulder made her stop. She had made little progress, and nowhere as much as the enemy boats. Her heart sank.

But just before she gave up in despair, she

felt her driftwood jerk forward. It was a gentle but definite nudge. And then her makeshift boat began to move all on its own. Except Emma knew it wasn't moving on its own; Pátzcuaro was helping.

"Thank you!" she whispered to the lake, and a squirt of water jumped up beside her before plopping back down with a little splash.

Now that she knew what was happening, Emma could brace herself more tightly, and the driftwood picked up speed. Before long she was zipping along at a much faster rate than the enemy boats, and if she weren't so worried about what she would find, Emma would have been laughing joyously at the ride. But she *was* worried. Because a lot of time had passed, and she could already see that the entire village was gathered on the beach, ready to fight their enemies.

Pátzcuaro led Emma to a little bay where

the waves were calm and the beach was empty. As soon as her driftwood got close enough to the shoreline that Emma could jump off, she splashed into the water. The tide receded, and she barely even got wet as she walked onto the beach.

Emma looked back at the enemy boats. Pátzcuaro was doing everything in his power to slow them down, making waves, whirlpools, and even splashing them with giant columns of water. But the enemy tribe was still making headway, and fast!

From where she was standing, Emma could clearly see the palace. She quickly made her way toward it, and from there she was able to find the stone prisons.

Emma crouched in the shrubbery, peeking out from behind some big leaves to check for guards. Surprisingly, there were none. Still, she waited a few beats to be triple sure, peering into all corners in case the guards were hidden from view. But after a minute she realized the prisons were entirely unguarded.

"Phew! That's good news," she said under her breath. Though a teeny-tiny pang of worry burned in her stomach. *Why are the prisons unguarded?*

Emma wasn't entirely sure which prison held Martín and which one held Abuela, so she approached the closest one.

"Martín? Abuela?" She peered inside. There was no answer.

Emma moved on to the next.

"Martín? Abuela?"

Nothing.

And the next.

"Martín? Abuela?

"Martín?

"Abuela?"

One by one, Emma went up to each stone

prison, looking for her brother and grandmother. With no success.

"Uh-oh . . ." She felt her stomach tighten. But she also knew she needed to keep calm in order to think straight.

Emma took a deep breath and tried to think of possible explanations. She knew there had to be a logical one, but none were coming to mind. All she could think about were terrible scenarios: that maybe she was too late, or maybe Hapunda's brothers had discovered Emma had left and punished Martín and Abuela; maybe the legend had kicked her brother and grandmother out when Emma went back home without them.

Emma was at a loss, and there was only one thing she could think to do.

She turned on her heels and ran as quickly as she could.

## A Giant Whirlpool!

From the top of the temple, Martín and Abuela had a good view of the guard that had taken the sticky hand. He flung it at an enemy warrior. The warrior jumped to get out of the way—right into one of Hapunda's brothers. The brother pushed the enemy warrior, and he fell into the lake with a splash. Pátzcuaro pulled him away from the shore, and the enemy warrior had to swim back to one of the boats.

"I can't believe that's actually working!" Martín grinned.

Abuela joined him in laughing. Then she pointed to the right. "Oh, look!" she said. "Is that Emma?"

It was Emma!

"She made it back!" Martín began waving his hands wildly to get her attention.

But Emma wasn't running toward them; she was running to the lake.

"Where is she going?" Martín wondered.

The answer became clear as soon as Emma reached the edge of the lake.

Martín saw a huge bubble begin to rise from the water, growing bigger

and bigger

and bigger

until it was as big as Emma!

"Whoa!" Martín whispered. Then a door

in the bubble seemed to open, and Hapunda stepped out.

Martín could see Emma and Hapunda talking. Emma seemed anxious—her hands were moving all over the place as she talked and she kept pointing over to the stone prisons.

"She doesn't know where we are," Abuela whispered. "Poor Emma. She must be so worried!"

Of course, Hapunda didn't know where they were, either, which explained why, instead of returning to her watery shelter, Hapunda began running with Emma straight toward the temple.

"Uh-oh!" Martín pointed at a boatful of enemies that had managed to reach the shore and were quickly jumping out onto the land.

"Emma and Hapunda are going to run right into them!" he told Abuela.

"You need to warn them," Abuela replied.

Martín was already running down the temple stairs before Abuela uttered her next word. "Hurry!"

"Emma!" Martín cried as he ran toward his sister. "Hapunda!"

The two girls spotted him and raced to meet him. Emma wrapped her arms so tightly around Martín that she almost knocked him over.

"Oh my gosh," she said. "I was so worried when I didn't see you! I had no idea what happened."

Martín quickly explained how the guards had taken them out of the prisons and brought them to the king.

"Ugh!" Hapunda groaned. "They're so hasty. They never listen to me. Just wait until I—"

But she couldn't finish her sentence because at that very moment, a huge net came down upon her, and Hapunda fell to her knees.

Emma gasped as a net fell over her, and

Martín had just enough time to take two steps before a third net trapped him.

The enemy tribe cheered as they surrounded Hapunda, Emma, and Martín, pulling them to their feet.

"No!" Martín cried. "Let us go!"

But the enemy was not going to let them go.

Just then one of Hapunda's brothers came running over. "Release our sister!"

An enemy soldier pulled Hapunda closer. "No. She is ours now."

"We will fight you to the death!" one of the brothers called.

"Then we will burn down your village."

Some of the warriors that had managed to get onto the shore were carrying torches.

"Stop!" Hapunda cried. "Please don't hurt anyone. I will go with you."

"Hapunda!" her brother cried. "We can't let them take you. It's our job to protect you."

She turned to her brothers. "I *was* protected, safe and well hidden," she told them. "Emma and Martín were telling the truth. If you hadn't been so mistrustful of them and made them your prisoners, I would still be hiding."

"Oh..." Her brothers looked a little ashamed.

The king arrived then, with Abuela at his side.

"My daughter," he cried. "I beg you, please don't take her!"

The king tried to pull Hapunda away, but the warrior next to Hapunda tightened his grip on her arm.

"Father," she said, "they have promised to spare the village if I go with them. You must let me go."

"But—" Tears spilled from the king's eyes.

"Let's go!" The enemy leader called out to everyone to get back on the boats. They dragged Hapunda toward one of the waiting boats. Someone helped take the nets off Emma and Martín, and they joined the tearful crowd on the shore.

Abuela tried to comfort the old king, who was crying inconsolably.

"You know who else is not going to be happy?" Martín whispered to Emma.

"Pátzcuaro," she said, and pointed to the middle of the lake, where a giant whirlpool was forming.

## A Feathery Transformation

Pátzcuaro had not been at all happy when Hapunda had left the safety of the water sphere. He begged her to stay, but Hapunda was worried about Martín and Abuela and angry at her brothers for what they had done.

Now, as Hapunda was being carried away by the enemy tribe, Emma knew that Pátzcuaro was not going to let them take her without a fight.

The enemy tribe was paddling as far away from the whirlpool as they could, but Pátzcuaro kept moving the whirlpool closer to them. The watery twister was making a loud splashing sound, like a giant waterfall crashing over rocks, as it pulled all the boats toward its center.

The enemy tribe was scared. Many of them jumped into the lake and began to swim away from the boats. But some of them stayed in their boats and were being pulled faster and faster into the spinning swirl.

"Oh dear," Abuela fretted.

"They're going to die!" Emma said.

"That will teach them," one of Hapunda's brothers replied.

It was too frightening to watch, and Emma turned away.

"Pátzcuaro, no!" she heard Hapunda cry. "That isn't the way to handle this."

Instantly, the sound of swirling water

stopped, and when Emma turned back to look, the lake was as still as a sheet of glass.

The king, Hapunda's brothers, and the villagers all gasped.

"How did she do that?" someone asked.

However, the enemy tribe didn't care. They just cheered and began paddling across the lake once more.

Hapunda dipped her hand into the lake, and Emma heard her say, "Thank you" as she dragged her fingers through the water.

Everyone was very quiet then and very sad as they watched the princess sail farther away. Even the sky was sad as clouds rolled over the lake, making everything gray and drizzly.

"I can't believe that's how this story ends," Martín leaned over and whispered to Emma.

Apparently, however, that was not how the story was going to end!

Just as Hapunda's boat was nearing the

shore, a long column of water shot out of the lake. The water arched toward Hapunda's boat, like a bridge, landing right next to the boat. The enemy tribe watched with their mouths hanging open.

Before the enemy could respond, Hapunda rose and stepped onto the archway of water. The water bridge pulled away from the boat.

"Come back here!" one of the enemy warriors called out. "If you don't come with us, we will burn down your village."

One boat began paddling back toward her. "We won't stop until we catch you."

"Then I will never let you catch me," Hapunda said, and she dove into the lake.

"After her!" an enemy warrior yelled, and a few people jumped into the water.

They dove and swam around, but nobody could find Hapunda.

"Where did she go?" their leader barked at

them, which was exactly what Emma was wondering.

"We can't find her anywhere," the swimming warriors said.

"Hapunda, my daughter!" the king began to wail. And Emma felt like she was about to cry too.

But just then the surface of the lake rippled, and out flew a beautiful white heron. Its neck was long and graceful, its beak the color of the sun. The heron extended its large wings and rose to the sky, circling the boats and then flying back toward the villagers watching on the shore.

The bird approached and landed in front of the king, gently tapping his arm.

"Hapunda?" the king asked, and the bird nodded.

"It *is* you!" The king wrapped his arms around the heron's neck.

Hapunda ruffled her feathers and nuzzled

against her father. Then she did the same with each of her brothers, Emma, Abuela, and Martín before spreading her wings and rising into the sky. This time a siege of herons rose from different parts of the lake. They joined Hapunda and flew as a group toward the enemy tribe.

The warriors in the water swam as quickly as possible back to their boats.

"Hurry. Row, row, row!" the leaders ordered, and the warriors began rowing as fast as they could.

Hapunda and the other birds flapped their wings and pecked at the boats. A few even poked the arms of some of the warriors. Eventually the birds pushed the enemy back to the shore. The enemy tribe ran into the forest as soon as their vessels touched the sand, not even bothering to pull up their boats. Still, Hapunda and her flock chased after them.

Meanwhile, the villagers cheered and clapped and shared hugs all around.

"She saved us!" they cried. "The princess saved us."

"Hooray!"

## Same but Different

"I'm so relieved," Abuela said. "I was worried for the young princess."

They waited for Hapunda to fly back.

Martín was the first to spot them. "Look!"

The heron princess was in the lead. Her feathers were so white that they seemed to be glowing. Behind her was a giant cloud of birds.

The birds all scattered back to the various

spots where they had been wading in the lake before the attack. Martín expected Hapunda to return to where he and the villagers were standing. But she didn't. Instead, she dove straight back into the water.

Everyone was confused and asking questions. Just then a wall of water rose in front of them in the shape of an oval glass. Inside it was a young man, and next to him was Hapunda.

"Hapunda!" everyone cried. "You're okay."

"I am," she told them. "Thanks to Pátzcuaro." She nodded at the young man next to her. "He turned me into a heron."

"You saved us!" one of Hapunda's brothers said. "It looks like the enemy won't ever be coming back."

Everyone cheered.

"You can turn back into my beautiful daughter now," the king said.

"Actually," Hapunda replied, "I can't. The transformation was permanent. I can only appear in my human form here, but that's just an illusion."

"Oh no!" Emma cried.

"That's terrible," said Martín.

"It's not really." Hapunda smiled. "I'm still me, the same Hapunda I was before. I'm just a little bit different now."

"A *lot* different," Martín whispered.

The king had begun to sob.

"Please don't cry," Hapunda told him. "We won this battle."

"What do you mean?" the king cried. "You're a bird!"

"But I get to be here with you. For the rest of my life. The enemy tribe thought they could decide my fate, but I ended up being in control."

And Hapunda's words activated a memory in Emma's mind.

"That's like what Dad told me!" she exclaimed.

"What?" said Martín, Abuela, the king, and about a dozen other people.

Emma blushed, but she explained about Dad's nugget of wisdom: . . . *determine what's in your control and what's not. Then change what you can, to make your situation better.*

"Hapunda had no control over whether or not the enemy tribe came for her," Emma explained. "But she changed what was in her control, and she made her situation better."

"I like that," the king said, and he wiped his tears.

Hapunda looked over at Pátzcuaro, and then her face got all lovey-dovey. Emma sighed, and everyone else was smiling and nodding. It was a bit much, Martín thought.

"Blech," he whispered, but apparently not quietly enough since Emma nudged him in the ribs.

"Well," the king said, "I would much rather have you here as a bird, living on the lake, than

off with those monsters!" He turned to the villagers. "And so tonight we celebrate!"

Everyone agreed and cheerfully began making their way back to the village center.

Only Abuela, Martín, and Emma stayed back.

"You are welcome to join the celebration," Hapunda told them.

"I'm afraid it's time for us to be getting back," Abuela replied. "These old bones have had enough adventure for one day." She turned to Martín and Emma. "Is that okay with you two?"

They both nodded.

"In that case..." Hapunda extended her hand out to them. On her palm were three clear and shimmering stones. "A gift, to remember us."

Abuela reached her hand into the watery mirror and plucked out the stones. She showed them to Emma and Martín.

"Wow. They look like diamonds," Emma said.

Martín thought they looked more like tiny

drops of water frozen into stone. The effect was very cool.

Each stone had a little silver loop at the top.

"I thought you might be able to wear them on your bracelets," Hapunda explained. "Like a charm."

"Oh, I love it!" Emma replied, and she slipped her stone onto her bracelet. "It looks beautiful. Thank you!"

After they said their goodbyes, it was just Abuela, Martín, and Emma left at the lake.

"It's so quiet now, isn't it?" Martín asked.

The sun was setting, and the sky was Martín's favorite color: a blue-purple combo that no matter how many times he tried to make with paint never turned out quite right.

There were already hundreds of stars, far more than Martín had ever seen, and they were all reflected on the lake.

"It's quite beautiful," Abuela said. "A perfect ending to a grand adventure."

She put one arm around Martín and another around Emma, pulling them all into a big three-way hug.

"Ready?" Emma asked. Martín nodded, and Emma reached for the obsidian necklace hanging around her neck. With her other hand, she touched the diamond-like gem hanging on her bracelet. Instantly, a portal opened before them.

## Lesson Learned

Floating right over the lake was the room Emma and Martín shared.

"Well." Abuela sighed, looking around. "I suppose I'll go first."

Abuela stepped into the room. Martín went next, and then Emma. The portal closed behind her. And it was perfect timing too, for not a second later there was a quick knock, and the door opened. Mami poked her head in.

"Oh, you're all here." She looked at them and then frowned. "You all look awfully suspicious. What are you—"

"Wow!" Abuela suddenly said. "Something smells absolutely delicious." She winked at Emma and Martín. "What are you making, mija?"

"Oh." Mami turned to Abuela. "Funny you should ask. I'm making chilaquiles. Your favorite!"

Abuela rubbed her tummy. "I can't wait. Can I help you?"

"Sure. I was actually coming to see if anyone wanted to join me in the kitchen."

"I'd love to!" Abuela took Mami's arm, and they walked out of Martín and Emma's room.

"That was a close one," Martín said. "Leave it to Abuela to get us out of it."

Emma laughed as she picked up the book of legends. The title page no longer had the tell-tale shell that indicated the legend was ready to be visited.

"It looks like we accomplished our mission," she told Martín.

"What do you think the legend was trying to teach us?" he asked.

"I think the lesson was mostly for me this time," she admitted. "You've already done a really good job at this."

"O-kay...?" Martín waited.

Emma explained. "Hapunda, like me, was put in a situation she didn't really like. And she couldn't change it; the enemy was coming whether she wanted them to or not."

"Like you?" Martín asked.

"Well, I keep wanting things to be different here, for this to be Mexico."

Martín nodded.

"But I know that's not possible," Emma said.

"Still," Martín said. "It's not like you can

turn into a bird to make things better."

"No. And also, that wouldn't actually make things better."

They both laughed at that.

"But I was thinking about something Dad said," Emma explained. "There are some things that are in my control, things I *can* do to make the situation here better."

"Like what?"

She told Martín about what she used to do in Mexico when there was a new student at the school. Then she added, "I was thinking I could make the first move and go talk to someone, but…"

"But what?" Martín asked.

"What would I say? It's not like I can just go up to someone and say, 'Hi, I'm Emma.' That would be so weird."

"Well, not *that* weird," Martín replied. "I do that all the time."

"You do? How? What do you talk about?"

"Well, why don't you start with someone in your class? Like someone at your table?"

"That's a good idea!" she said.

"And, I don't know," Martín continued. "I suppose you could tell them about that goofy thing I did when we went to get ice cream one time?"

Emma frowned. "*What* goofy thing? When did we go get ice cream?"

Martín grinned. "The goofy thing I'm going to do today after we go get ice cream so that you have something to talk about with your table partner."

Emma returned his grin. "I'm sure Mami and Dad will approve."

"And I have another idea," Martín went on.

"Is it as good as your ice cream one?" Emma asked.

"Yep. Why don't you try to find one thing

that you think is cool every day?" he explained. "It doesn't have to be a big deal or especially awesome. But then at dinner we can swap cool things and see which one is the coolest."

"You're just turning this into a contest so that I participate," she said.

"Maybe." He shrugged. "So?"

"Fine." She thought back through her day, her mind lingering on Mami's chat with Mrs. Grundi and the butterscotch candy and how the people in line at the bakery were so friendly and chatting with the cashier.

"I guess one thing I do like," she began, "is how friendly everyone is in our neighborhood."

"That's true," Martín said.

People were friendly in Mexico, too, but she liked how quickly her family had been accepted in their new community. "And if I had to say another thing..." Emma continued.

By the time Mami called them down to dinner, Emma and Martín had swapped at least six cool things they liked about living in the US. And for the first time in a long time, Emma wasn't one bit annoyed at her brother. That was definitely a welcome change!

"Thanks," she said, and she gave Martín a big hug before heading down to dinner.

## Author's Note

This story is based on a P'urhépecha legend about the origin of Lake Pátzcuaro. The P'urhépecha people are a pre-Hispanic Indigenous group that once lived in Mexico's southwestern state of Michoacán. Between the fourteenth and early sixteenth centuries, P'urhépecha had an estimated population of more than one million people. They chose to settle in the Lake Pátzcuaro basin due to its many habitable islands, bountiful waters, and the lush green landscape surrounding the lake.

As with most legends, there are many variations of this tale. My favorite comes from David Bowles's book, *Feathered Serpent, Dark Heart of Sky: Myths of Mexico*.

# Acknowledgments

Aladdin magic makers who helped create this book:

Adventurous Agent: Ammi-Joan Paquette

Visionary Illustrator: Vanessa Morales

Publisher: Valerie Garfield

Associate Publisher: Anna Jarzab

Editor: Anna Parsons

Designer: Tiara Iandiorio

Production Manager: Sara Berko

Production Editor: Nicole Tai

Copyeditor: Penina Lopez

Proofreader: Elizabeth Brooke Littrell

Cold Reader: Jasmine Ye

Marketing Director: Caitlin Sweeny

Marketing Manager: Alissa Rashid